ABOUT THE AUTHOR

Christopher Pike was born in New York, but grew up in Los Angeles, where he still lives. Prior to becoming a writer, he worked in a factory, painted houses and programmed computers. His hobbies include astronomy, meditating, running and making sure his books are prominently displayed in his local bookshop. As well as being a best-selling children's writer, he is also the author of three adult novels.

Spooksville

Spooksville

PHONE FEAR

Christopher Pike

**Hodder
Children's
Books**

a division of Hodder Headline plc

First published in Great Britain in 1998
by Hodder Children's Books
a division of Hodder Headline plc
338 Euston Road
London NW1 3BH

A Catalogue record for this book is available from the British Library

ISBN 0 340 68630 8

Typeset by Avon Dataset Ltd, Bidford-on-Avon, Warks

Printed and bound in Great Britain by
Mackays of Chatham, Chatham, Kent

One

The gang were sitting in their favourite doughnut shop when the first threatening call came. The call was for Bryce Poole – he was the only one who carried a cellular phone at all times. Of course none of them, at first, worried much about the weird call. They had faced so many dangers living in Spooksville, they thought they were invincible. Besides, they were sure it was just a crank call. What none of them realised was that they were about to come face to face with the greatest evil ever to threaten mankind.

Yet it did not have a face, not until later.

Then it was a face they gave it, a face they made.

'It's almost summer,' Sally Wilcox said as she sipped her extra-strong black coffee and munched on a jam doughnut. Sally was addicted to coffee, to the caffeine probably, and it suited her. Sally was a high wired act, always talking, thinking, acting – she had an opinion on everything. She was tall and thin, with long dark hair and dark eyes. She added, 'What are we going to do when we get out of school?'

'I think we should concentrate on using the interdimensional portal in the cemetery and try to re-establish contact with some of our alien friends,' Bryce Poole said. Bryce had dark hair and colouring like Sally, and was now as tall as her, thanks to a year of rapid growth. He was serious and sometimes acted like he knew everything, but the gang had grown to like him and depend on him. In a crisis – which happened about every day in Spooksville – he was very resourceful.

'I like the idea of having more alien contact,' Watch said. 'But the portal in the graveyard has always been unpredictable.' Watch was the largest one in the group, with lighter hair and colouring. He was also probably the smartest – he had solved many next-to-impossible mysteries in the last two years. But he was something of a loner; he had no

2

family in Spooksville, and he seldom expressed his true feelings. His name was a nickname – he was fond of wearing four watches at once.

'The portal has taken us to some pretty dangerous places,' Adam Freeman said. Adam was relatively new to Spooksville, two years and counting, but he had finally begun to adjust to the town. When push came to shove, he was usually the one who decided what they should do next. For that reason the gang saw him as their leader. He was shorter than the others, with light brown hair and brown eyes. Adam added, 'I mean, it's taken us into dinosaur land and even down to hell. I think we should leave it alone.'

'Those demons were a pain in the butt,' Watch said.

'I think we should try to have fun this summer doing normal things,' Cindy Makey added. Like Adam, Cindy had lived in Spooksville for two years, but she wasn't sure she would ever get used to the place. Cindy was no coward, but it seemed that every time she turned around she was fighting for her life. It was beginning to get predictable, in her opinion. Cindy had blonde hair and blue eyes and a beautiful face, which she was trying to keep intact.

'Normal things would bore us,' Sally said.

'I don't get bored easily,' Cindy said. 'I enjoy my own company.'

'It's lucky someone does,' Sally remarked.

'Here they go again,' Adam muttered.

Cindy sat up, set down her doughnut, and glared at Sally.

'You just have to keep running around talking your mouth off because you have no inner peace,' Cindy said.

Sally shrugged. 'Who can have peace in a world as wicked as this one?'

'The reason the world is wicked is because people don't know how to relax,' Cindy shot back. 'People like you.'

Sally was annoyed. 'I know how to relax, I just don't enjoy it, that's all. Besides, lazy people like you cause most of the wickedness.'

'How dare you call me lazy!' Cindy retorted.

'How dare you call me wicked!' Sally said.

'I didn't say that. You're twisting my words!' Cindy went on.

'And you're twisting mine!' Sally said.

Adam put up his hands. 'You are both wonderful young women: full of energy, relaxation, and peace. Now can you both calm down so that we can finish our breakfast?'

Sally huffed. 'OK. No problem.'

Cindy returned to her milk. 'She started it.'

'Shh,' Adam cautioned. 'You both started it.'

'Anyway,' Watch said, not missing a beat, 'I think further alien contact should be at the top of our list of priorities this summer. I would also like to do more time travel. There are, I believe, certain historical facts that, if we could alter them, would make this world a much better place to live in.'

'If we go back in time again and change the past,' Sally interrupted, 'one of us might cease to exist in the present.'

Cindy smiled at her. 'I think that's what he means about making the world a better place to be – Ms Non-existent.'

Sally, fortunately, did not take the bait. She continued to sip her coffee.

'If we *do* go back in time,' Sally said, 'I want to get rid of the great-great-great-grandfather and grandmother of the guy who invented coffee.

Nowadays I have to drink six cups a day just to feel normal.'

'This is normal?' Cindy asked.

Bryce's cellular phone beeped. He picked it up with his right hand and put it to his ear. Sally made a face.

'He is *so* important,' she muttered.

'Hello?' Bryce said. He listened for a moment, then said, 'Who is this?'

They watched his face. He frowned slightly.

'Who's calling, please?' he said, stronger this time.

'Who is it?' Adam asked.

Bryce put his hand over the phone and whispered.

'Some weirdo,' he said.

'What does he want?' Cindy asked.

Bryce removed his hand from the phone and listened some more. His expression darkened and he looked annoyed.

'Yeah,' he said in response to whatever he was being told. 'I don't think so. I don't think I need to do anything you say. In fact, I'm hanging up right now.' Bryce clicked off the phone and set it face down on the table. 'Dumb,' he muttered.

'Who was it?' Cindy asked.

Bryce shrugged. 'I don't know, some nut. He said his name was Nernit, and that if I didn't do what he wanted I would be hurt.'

'What did he want you to do?' Sally asked.

Bryce was disgusted. 'He wanted me to take a baseball bat and break all the windows at Mr Warner's house, on Pickering.'

'But Mr Warner is such a nice man,' Cindy said. He was her postman, and always had a smile for everyone. She couldn't imagine anyone having a grudge against him.

'He's not that nice,' Sally said. 'He has a nasty habit of reading my personal mail.'

Adam snorted. 'When did you ever receive personal mail?'

Sally was insulted. 'I have many admirers in places that none of you guys know about.'

'Did Nernit say anything else?' Watch asked Bryce.

Bryce considered. 'He said something about being all-powerful and all-knowing. And that I had to obey him immediately or he would know.' Bryce paused and frowned again. 'He didn't have a normal voice.'

'What do you mean?' Adam asked.

'He sounded like a machine,' Bryce said.

Sally was not impressed. 'You can buy those devices in magic shops for ten bucks. They make you sound like a robot when you speak.'

Bryce nodded. 'Yeah, he sounded like he was using one of those things. I think he was trying to creep me out.'

Watch nodded at Bryce's phone. 'Hit star sixty-nine, and see if you can have your phone call back his number.'

Bryce did as he was told but then shook his head.

'The call isn't going through,' he said. 'Nernit must have it blocked.'

'Interesting,' Watch muttered.

'It's just a prank call, don't you think?' Adam said.

'Probably,' Watch said. 'Nernit certainly doesn't sound like a real name. But I think we should warn Mr Warner that someone has threatened him. Just in case.'

They all agreed that it was better to be safe than

sorry. Yet as they left the doughnut shop and lazily walked towards Mr Warner's house, none of them felt the slightest fear. The morning was warm and clear. Soon vacation time would be on them and they would have twelve free weeks to explore and play. They probably all felt, after all the times they had saved the world, that they deserved a vacation.

They didn't make it to Mr Warner's house.

A van came around the block, fast.

For some reason, Bryce was walking by himself. Walking behind them, probably not thinking about the threat.

Adam saw the van, but saw it too late.

'Bryce!' he screamed.

The van – it was black with silver chrome – put its driver's side tyres up on the pavement and accelerated. Bryce barely had a chance to look up before it was upon him. Yet at the last moment, perhaps by instinct, he jumped to the side. But it was not enough to save him. The corner bumper of the van hit him with a sickening thump. Bryce was thrown hard towards a row of bushes, his body spinning in midair as if he were made of straw.

The van didn't try for any more of them. It

immediately swerved off the pavement and back on to the road, perhaps being *careful* not to hit any of them. But it didn't matter, it had made its point. Bryce lay hurt and gasping for air on top of the bushes.

The weird voice on the phone hadn't been kidding.

Nernit was for real.

Two

They gathered around Bryce to help him but it was only Adam who had the good sense to stop the others from touching him. He had to hold them back.

'His back might be broken,' Adam said hastily. 'His neck. If we move him we might press a bone chip against his spinal cord and paralyse him.'

Cindy was crying. 'He's going into shock, we have to do something!'

'He's dying!' Sally shouted.

Bryce was breathing hard and had turned the colour of a bed sheet, but somehow he managed a smile.

'I am *not* going into shock and I am *not* dying. But I think my left leg is broken.'

Adam took a step forward and gently touched Bryce's left leg. Bryce groaned and Adam's face was grim.

'It doesn't feel good,' Adam said. 'He needs an ambulance.'

'No,' Sally pleaded. 'You know what Spooksville's hospital is like. The head surgeon doubles as the town undertaker. He has a vested interest in making his patients die. Bryce is better off with us.'

Adam turned to Watch. 'What do you think?'

Watch considered. 'When we were fighting the vampires Dr Paine helped us out. He wasn't so bad. I think he can be trusted to help Bryce.'

'If he's still alive,' Sally said. 'All the good doctors at Spooksville Memorial and up embalmed.'

Adam knelt by Bryce, who was barely supported by the bushes.

'Do you want to go to the hospital?' he asked gently.

Bryce tried to hide his pain but it was obvious that he was in agony. Sweat poured down his face and he had trouble speaking.

'I think I have to go *somewhere*,' he gasped. 'I can't lie in these bushes all day.'

'They probably won't try to fix the leg,' Sally warned. 'They'll probably just amputate.'

'Would you please shut up!' Cindy told her.

Sally went quiet. 'What did I say?'

'Then it's settled,' Adam said as he stood up. 'We call for an ambulance and we make sure Dr Paine treats him.'

'Where did that doctor get such a ridiculous name?' Sally muttered.

They called for an ambulance on Bryce's cell phone. The hospital responded quickly, but sent a hearse instead of ambulance, which did nothing to soothe their fears. Yet the man in black who drove the vehicle loaded Bryce into the back with great care, and even let them climb in with their friend. They tried to ignore the fact that he was extremely pale, seven feet tall, and had long sharp teeth. Cindy held Bryce's hand as he lay back on the red draped stretcher.

'You're going to be fine,' she told him.

Bryce managed another smile. 'I feel better already.'

'Just one thing. We can't let them put him under anaesthetic,' Sally warned. 'They use formaldehyde instead of chloroform.' She glanced quickly at the others. 'I'm not joking.'

'Nernit wasn't either,' Watch remarked, thoughtfully.

Fortunately, for their peace of mind, Dr Paine was the first one to greet them at the hospital. He was about sixty and looked like he had never learned to smile. He had silver eyebrows so bushy a nesting bird might have found them attractive. But like before he impressed them as someone who knew what he was doing, and as he wheeled Bryce to the examination room, they felt no need to follow. Dr Paine said he would fix up their friend and they believed him.

They sat in the waiting room – it was black and there were grinning skeletons with needles in their bony hands painted on the walls – and talked about Nernit and his attack.

'He probably has people under him,' Watch observed. 'He moved so fast after Bryce refused his offer.'

'So you don't think Nernit was driving the van that hit Bryce?' Adam asked.

Watch shook his head. 'I didn't see who was

driving, so I can't be sure. Probably like the rest of you, I was too busy watching Bryce fly through the air. But that black van – I have seen it around town before.'

'So this dude is a local,' Sally muttered.

'Not necessarily,' Watch said. 'And that's my point. He probably isn't working alone. You see, Bryce was hit minutes after we left the doughnut shop. I think we were being watched the whole time and that's not easy for one person to do.'

'But what is this guy's motive in bringing Bryce into his revenge?' Cindy asked. 'If he has people working for him, why didn't he just use them to go after Mr Warner without calling Bryce?'

'We always assume when there is violence that revenge must be a motive,' Watch said. 'But often the most violent people in society need no motive. They just hurt people because they like to hurt people.'

'We need to talk to Mr Warner, see if he can give us more information,' Adam said.

Sally nodded. 'Let's go and see him as soon as we know Bryce is OK. If he's still alive, that is,' she added.

Watch frowned. 'It still bothers me that this Nernit used a voice distortion device.'

'I don't find that odd,' Adam said. 'He probably doesn't want to be identified later. It's even possible that we know this guy. In fact, he might have altered his voice because Bryce might have recognised him right away.'

'It's possible,' Watch said, but he sounded unconvinced.

They had to wait a long time before Dr Paine reappeared, but thankfully the news was good. He said that Bryce had broken his leg, it had been set, and that he should make a full recovery. They asked to see him but Dr Paine wanted him to rest for a couple of hours. Apparently the doctor had given him painkillers, but they would wear off soon. He told them to come back later in the day and they thanked him for his help.

They weren't sure what to do about Nernit. But talking to Mr Warner and finding the black van seemed reasonable steps. Because it was a Sunday they knew the postman wouldn't be working. From the hospital to his house was only a fifteen minute walk. His car was parked out front. Yet when they knocked, there was no answer. They stood on the front porch and wondered what that meant.

'He could be out for a walk,' Adam offered.

'Why would a postman who walks all week go for a walk in his spare time?' Sally asked. She gestured to the car. 'I think he's inside, dead or alive.'

'We can't just break in,' Cindy said.

'Let's go round the back and peek in the windows,' Watch suggested. 'I don't want to leave here not knowing any more than when we came.'

There was a white picket fence and gate around the garden, but they were able to get over it easily. Mr Warner kept a tidy place, for a bachelor. Yet they didn't get to enjoy his well-trimmed lawn and bushes. They were scarcely in the garden when a gunshot rang out and one of the windows exploded. Glass sprinkled all around them and they hit the ground fast.

'Go away!' a voice shouted from inside. 'You're not going to get me!'

Adam raised his head from the grass. 'We just want to talk!'

Another shot rang out and another window exploded.

'Get out of my garden or I'll kill you!' Mr Warner yelled.

'He sounds scared,' Watch muttered.

'He's not the only one,' Sally gasped. 'He's lost his mind, we can't talk to him. I say we get out of here now before his aim improves.'

'For once I have to agree with Sally,' Cindy said.

Watch nodded reluctantly. 'I hate to say it but he does sound insane.'

Adam carefully got up on his knees. 'Don't shoot!' he called out. 'We're leaving right now! But we still want to talk, Mr Warner. This is Adam Freeman. Please call me later if you're feeling better.'

'You don't fool *me*!' Mr Warner shouted back. 'You're working for him! But I'm not working for him any more! And you can't make me! I don't care what you do to me!'

Watch also got up on his knees. 'But we're *not* working for him. Why, just a couple of hours ago one of our best friends was run down by a—'

A third shot rang out and the shirt sleeve on Watch's left arm tore open. Mr Warner meant business. They all leapt to their feet and dashed for the side of the house. They practically burst through the gate, and didn't stop running until they were round the block and out of breath. It was only then that they noticed Watch was bleeding. But he waved away their concern.

'The bullet grazed me,' he said. 'It'll stop bleeding in a few minutes.'

Adam shook his head. 'That was close. I wonder why he was acting so strange.'

'I think he half told us,' Watch said. 'Mr Warner has obviously received a call from Nernit. And from the sound of it he must have done what Nernit said in the past. But now he's chosen not to listen to him any more, and he's terrified what revenge Nernit will take. Nernit's order to Bryce must have been to scare Mr Warner further.'

Cindy was impressed. Your deductive powers are awesome.

'Any fool could have figured that out,' Sally muttered.

Adam spoke to Watch. 'So you think Nernit controls people by fear?'

'Yes,' Watch said. 'And if he fails to get someone

to do what he wants, he goes to another person and gets them to threaten the last person.'

'But why?' Cindy asked.

'I don't know,' Watch said. He paused in thought. 'I wonder why Bryce was contacted instead of one of us?'

'That may have been a coincidence,' Sally said. 'Nernit may be contacting people at random.'

They still had Bryce's cell phone with them. It beeped. Adam was carrying it.

They all stared at it, and at each other, before Adam picked it up. They huddled close so that they could hear. Adam pushed the receive button.

'Hello?' he said.

The voice was weirder than they had imagined. It sounded both human and mechanical, crazy and cold. It was low, the others had to strain to hear, and it spoke slowly.

'This is Nernit. You are Adam Freeman. You are in trouble. You have troubled me. You have obstructed my wishes. For this crime you may be punished. But you may avoid punishment by doing what I command. Do you understand?'

'Yes,' Adam said calmly. 'What do you command?'

'Listen. In your town there is a certain Mrs Baker. She lives at 412 Morse Street. She's home right now and she's alone. To avoid punishment, you are to go to her house immediately and set it on fire. You are to trap her inside so that she will perish in the fire.'

'Don't be ridiculous,' Adam said. 'There's no way I'll do that.'

The voice went on without changing tone.

'Your friend Bryce Poole chose to disobey me. You saw what happened to him. Are you anxious to be punished as well?'

'I'm not anxious to be punished,' Adam said. 'I just think you're a real strange character who needs to be caught and locked up.'

'I cannot be caught. I cannot be locked up. You will be punished.'

'Go ahead, do what you want, I don't care.'

Nernit did not hesitate.

'You will care,' the voice said.

The connection broke and they heard static. Watch took the phone from Adam's hand and listened to the sound.

'That's odd,' Watch said. 'It is not like he

21

just hung up. It sounds different.'

'Careful,' Sally said. 'He might be able to still hear us.'

Watch glanced around. 'Nernit knew Adam was the one who held the cell phone. He called him by name. That means we're being watched right now.'

They studied the row of quiet houses, the many windows, but saw no one. Yet they were scared now, Nernit had sounded so strange and he obviously had great power.

'He didn't say how Adam would be hurt,' Cindy muttered.

'If he stays true to his pattern he'll attack soon,' Watch said.

'I'm not afraid,' Adam said.

'Of course you are,' Sally said. 'You're terrified.'

'We have to get Adam inside,' Cindy said. 'Hide him out of the way.'

Watch was doubtful. 'No. Nernit had no scruples about attacking Mrs Baker inside her own home. We are not going to defeat this guy by running and hiding.'

'We are not going to defeat him by dying,' Sally said.

'We have to contact Mrs Baker and warn her that Nernit plans to burn her house down,' Cindy said. 'Let's do that first so that at least she can try to get out of town.'

'We don't know how far this guy's influence reaches,' Watch said. 'No town may be safe.'

They headed for 412 Morse Street. None of them were surprised when they knocked on Mrs Baker's door and they got no response. They weren't about to sneak into her garden. Adam called out loud enough so that if she was inside she could hear what he had to say.

'Mrs Baker,' he said. 'We know you're in there and probably too scared to answer. We don't blame you, we've been talking to Nernit as well. He ordered us to come here and burn your house down with you inside. Now, you don't have to worry, we're not going to do it. But we told him that, so it's possible that he's sending someone else over right now. We think you should get out of town and go somewhere where no one knows who you are. Also, stay away from phones.'

There was no clear response from inside.

But Adam thought he heard a faint shriek.

Mrs Baker was an old woman with poor eyesight.

It made the whole gang want to get Nernit all the more.

They were walking back to Adam's house when they were attacked.

Three

Nernit's punishment was at first not as dramatic as it had been with Bryce. No speeding vehicle swung round the corner and tried to mow Adam down. The gang were simply walking down the pavement, with Adam in the centre, when they approached a blonde girl about their own age. She had a fresh, innocent face, and although they had not seen her before around town, she looked like the last person who would hurt someone.

Yet they should have looked closer. The girl was pretty, but she was tense. Her eyes were slightly bloodshot – she had probably been crying. Most of all it was the way she carried herself that should have set off alarms. It was a warm day but she had on a long dark coat and had both her hands hidden deep in her coat pockets.

Yet it wasn't until she was three metres away that they noticed her.

That was when she pulled out a knife. The blade glittered in the afternoon sun. It was long and silver and they didn't have to study it closely to know it was sharp.

She didn't say a word.

She raised the knife and lunged towards Adam.

It was clear she meant to stab him in the heart.

Adam didn't react. He saw the knife and seemed to freeze.

It was Sally who saved the day. With no thought for her own safety she jumped in front of Adam. Yet Sally was no fool, she had no intention of taking the stab for Adam. In a swift move she kicked at the girl's right knee, hard. Sally's aim was spot-on. There was a faint cracking sound and the girl let out a sharp cry, dropped the knife, and fell to the ground. She rolled in front of them on the pavement like a broken doll. Cindy kicked the knife aside and high-fived Sally.

It was nice to see the two girls smile at each other.

Even though Adam had nearly been killed.

Watch knelt by the fallen girl and grabbed her hand.

'You don't have to be afraid,' he said. 'We know Nernit sent you to kill our friend and we don't hold it against you.'

'Speak for yourself,' Sally said. 'This girl must be a coward to even think of doing Nernit's bidding.'

From her place on the ground, holding her injured knee, the girl glared at Sally. 'I'm no coward,' she said. 'I have defied him longer than you know.'

Adam also knelt by the girl and helped her into a sitting position.

'What's your name?' he asked. 'Where are you from?'

She sat up slowly and continued to rub her knee.

'I'm Savannah Stranger,' she said. 'I live in Florence, thirty kilometres south of here.' She looked at them anxiously. 'What are you guys going to do with me?'

'Probably slice you open with your own knife and roast your skin on our barbecue,' Sally said.

'We're on your side,' Watch said calmly. 'But you need to help us. Did you get a call from Nernit in the last hour to come here and hurt Adam?'

'I got a call early this morning,' Savannah said.

'But I hadn't even talked to Nernit then,' Adam said. 'Neither had Bryce.'

'Yet Nernit told you to come here specifically and hurt Adam?' Watch asked Savannah.

'Yes,' Savannah said. 'But he told me to wait until he beeped me, which he did twenty minutes ago.'

'You've been following us all day?' Cindy asked.

'Yes.'

Sally snorted. 'Then you saw what your Nernit did to our friend. And you still agreed to help him?'

Savannah spoke bitterly. 'I didn't *agree* to help him. I'm being forced to help him.' Her face broke and she lowered her head. She wept quietly. 'He's going to kill my brother, Clay, if I don't do what he says. Do you understand?'

'When did Nernit first contact you?' Watch asked carefully.

Savannah looked up. 'A month ago. The first time, he ordered me to spray paint all the windows at school. I thought it was a crank call so I ignored him.' Her voice faltered. 'Then he punished me.'

'What did he do?' Adam asked.

She wiped her eyes. 'I don't want to talk about it – it was horrible. But after that I began to do what he said.'

'So you've killed lots of people?' Sally said.

Savannah was annoyed. 'I haven't killed anyone. Today was the first time he gave me such an order. Usually I just have to set a house on fire or else blow up a car.'

'That's not so bad,' Sally said.

'Would you really have killed me?' Adam asked.

Savannah stared at him. Her eyes were a clear blue, despite her tears; her shoulder-length blonde hair was shiny. She really was a beautiful girl. Adam figured if someone had to kill him, he could have done much worse. Savannah shook her head in response to his question.

'I just planned to cut you, make you bleed,' she said. 'Then I was going to try to convince Nernit that I had done my best.'

'Does Nernit ever take excuses?' Watch asked.

Savannah lowered her head again. 'No.'

Cindy was sympathetic. 'So your brother is in danger?'

Savannah nodded weakly. 'I know we're being watched even now. Nernit will know I've failed. He won't wait long before he sends someone after Clay.' She tried to stand. 'I have to get back home and protect him.'

Watch helped her up but stopped her.

'You won't be able to protect him if what you say is true,' Watch told her. 'Your best hope is to stick with us and help us defeat this guy.'

Savannah tried not to snigger but was not entirely successful.

'You guys think you can defeat Nernit?' she asked. 'You don't stand a chance. He has thousands working for him. They will come for you and they will kill you. If not today, then tomorrow. Do you understand?'

'How do you know he has thousands under him?' Watch asked.

Savannah shook her head. 'It is obvious, that's all. I haven't done anything this last month without him knowing about it.'

'But who is he?' Sally demanded.

Savannah glanced nervously around. 'No one knows for sure. But it's said that he isn't human. That he's some kind of demonic spirit sent here to punish us for our sins.'

'You must be all of twelve years old,' Sally said. 'What sins have you committed?'

Savannah wanted to leave. 'I don't know and it doesn't matter. I'm under his control and I have to accept that. But now I've disobeyed him and either me or my brother will have to pay. You must let me go, I need to get home and warn my brother.'

'Does he know about Nernit?' Adam asked.

'No,' Savannah said. 'He knows nothing.'

'You can warn your brother on the phone.' Watch said. 'Tell him to get out of town.'

'You don't understand,' Savannah pleaded. 'That won't make any difference. Nernit will still find him.'

Watch shook his head. 'I believe this guy is powerful but I don't think he's omnipotent. And he's no demon.'

'What do you know?' Savannah said.

Sally was offended. 'Listen, girl, if you knew who you were talking to, you would treat us with more respect. We live in Spooksville, and face witches, aliens, vampires and dinosaurs on a regular basis. We always come out ahead. This Nernit guy doesn't scare us, we'll take care of him the same way we take care of all troublemakers.'

Savannah stared at her and then smiled. But it was a sad smile and it was obvious to the rest of them that she was under great pressure.

'If you're not scared now,' Savannah said, 'you soon will be.' She glanced at Watch. 'Will you let me go?'

Watch took a step back. 'We're not holding you. But listen to what I have to say. Sally isn't boasting. We really *are* resourceful. We can beat this guy, as soon as we find out who he is and what he wants. But we need your help, you've had much more experience with him than us.'

Savannah shook her head. 'I don't know any more about him than you. I told you, he's a complete mystery. You just hear his voice on the phone and that's it.'

'But there will be little things you know that we don't,' Watch said. 'You don't know what they are right now and neither do we. But they'll come up as we work together. And we've found that it's the little things that matter. We need to gather as many clues as possible.'

'He's right,' Adam said to Savannah. 'Stay with us, for your own safety. Your brother must trust you. If you tell him to get out of town, he will. How old is he?'

'Sixteen.'

Sally laughed. 'And he needs *you* to take care of *him*? Boy, he's old enough to drive a car.'

Savannah considered. 'Do you guys have a plan of action?'

'We're working on one,' Adam said.

'Great,' she muttered doubtfully.

Watch spoke. 'Savannah, I'm curious. Each time Nernit has spoken to you, has his voice sounded mechanical?'

'Yes.'

'Why are you so hung up on the mechanical thing?' Sally asked. 'It's obvious he's using a voice distortion device.'

'That is one obvious deduction,' Watch said. 'But what may be even more obvious is that his voice is simply mechanical.'

They were all astounded.

'Are you saying that this guy is a robot?' Adam asked.

'I'm not sure,' Watch said. 'But I don't want to dismiss the possibility.'

'But there are no robots,' Savannah said. 'It's a crazy idea.'

'Not only are there robots in this galaxy,' Sally assured her. 'But there are also many other types of creatures you cannot even imagine. We've met many of them.'

Savannah looked at her doubtfully. 'You guys sound as crazy as Nernit.'

'It takes a crazy person to defeat a crazy person,' Sally said gamely.

'Let's take a step back,' Watch said. 'Nernit told Savannah to come up here early this morning. Now clearly he knew he was going to order Bryce to break Mr Warner's windows, and that Bryce would refuse. Then, to take it a step further, he must have known he would contact Adam next and that Adam would refuse to do his bidding.'

'The guy is smart – what's your point?' Sally asked.

'I'm saying he knew something of Bryce's character,' Watch said, 'as well as Adam's character. Now what do these two have in common?'

'They're both righteous dudes?' Sally said.

'What *do* we have in common?' Adam asked.

Watch shrugged. 'I don't know all the answers. I am just posing the questions so that we can get going in the right direction. But let's suppose for a moment that Nernit sounds mechanical because he *is* mechanical. Then let us all agree that he knows a lot about you guys, or at least enough to know you won't jump just because he gives you an order. Where could he have got this information?'

'But if he is a demon he might just know,' Cindy said.

Watch waved his hand. 'Let's stick with the facts and think.'

'This is Spooksville,' Sally warned. 'In this town there are facts and there are facts. It's possible that he is some kind of supernatural being. In that case we're probably all doomed.'

'But this Nernit is not confined to Spooksville,' Adam pointed out. 'He could be all over the world, for all we know.'

'My point exactly,' Watch said. 'And if he is all over the world, and he is mechanical, and he knows about certain people, who – or what – is he?'

Adam shrugged. 'The only thing like that is the Internet.'

Watch smiled. 'Yes. That's what I was thinking. The Internet links the world, it is made up of machines and has tons of information on people. In fact, both you and Bryce are online all the time. And I have a sneaking suspicion that Savannah is online as well. Is that true?'

She stared at him in wonder. 'You guys really are smart.'

'We try our best,' Sally said humbly.

Savannah nodded. 'Yes, I've been online for a year now. But millions of people are. Besides, what are you saying? The Internet is a bunch of computers spread all over the world. The only thing that connects them are people's modem lines.'

Watch nodded. 'It's true that the Internet is nothing but computers and modem lines. But modem lines use phones. The only way Nernit contacts people is over the phone. Also, computers can talk these days. There are all kinds of voice recognition devices out there, and mechanical voice generators. Like I said, I think Nernit sounds mechanical because he is mechanical.'

'But you're still not saying what he is,' Savannah said. 'Nernit is a murderer. The Internet is harmless.'

'We *assume* it's harmless, we're not sure,' Watch said. 'But I'm not saying Nernit is precisely the Internet. It reminds me of a line from one of my favourite movies, *Terminator*. The hero is trying to explain to the heroine how the defence computer system in the United States destroys the world. This movie came out before there was an Internet. Anyway, he says how there are all these computers interconnected and how sophisticated they are. Then he says this chilling line; "*They say it got smart.*" '

'You're saying that somewhere buried in the Internet a creature became conscious?' Adam asked.

'Exactly,' Watch said. 'These interconnected computers have taken the place of its brain cells. Probably when a critical mass of chips was achieved, consciousness dawned. Then the thing began to call people using the modem lines.'

'That is such a weird idea,' Savannah said, but she was listening.

'More weird than an all-powerful demon?' Watch asked.

'But why would this creature be so hostile?' Cindy asked. 'If it knows so much about people, why is it trying to hurt them?'

'I think it's better to ask if it was created out of its storehouse of knowledge of people,' Watch said. 'If you go online for any length of time you meet a lot of sick people, particularly late at night. It may be ironic, but Nernit might be hostile because he *is* so human.'

Savannah shook her head. 'I don't know if I buy any of this. You're saying this person, this creature, appeared out of nothing?'

'No,' Watch said. 'It appeared in the midst of the most complex computer system in the world. Not in the midst of nothing. Also, there's another clue, and it may be the definitive one. We pronounce Nernit's name the way he does and we probably mentally spell it in its simplest form, N–E–R–N–I– T. But if we add an E beside the other E and we tack a T on to the last T we still have a spelling that can be pronounced the way he says his name.'

'What's your point?' Sally asked.

'N–E–E–R–N–I–T–T is probably how he spells his own name,' Watch said, 'Think about it for a minute. That spelling is an anagram of the word Internet.'

'You're right!' Adam exclaimed.

'You are so smart,' Savannah said again in awe.

'What's an anagram?' Sally muttered.

'The letters are changed round to form another word,' Cindy explained.

'I knew that,' Sally said quickly. 'I just wanted to see if you knew.'

'Oh no,' Savannah said. 'If this is true, and he is in the Internet, then we can *never* destroy him. The Internet's computers and modem lines are scattered all over the world.'

'But if I'm right,' Watch said, 'it does mean one good thing.'

'What's that?' Adam asked.

'We can talk to him,' Watch said.

'How?' Sally asked.

'We can go online and call him,' Watch said simply.

Four

They went to Watch's house, which was empty because Watch lived alone. The gang knew Watch had family but for some reason they were scattered all over the country. But because the gang were sensitive to his feelings, they didn't pry about the matter.

Watch had an assortment of computers, one in every room in his house. He booted a PC and got online. Then came the big difficulty.

How to get Neernitt's attention?

'It's not like he's in some chat room somewhere,' Sally said. 'I doubt he has a web page.'

'I disagree, in a sense,' Watch said as he sat in front of the computer screen with the rest of them gathered round. 'I think he may be in *every* chat

41

room in the world. I know he has access to every web page that has ever been constructed. I think he may have been eavesdropping on many people before making a move.'

'You're saying his consciousness isn't localised?' Adam asked. 'He can tap into many conversations at once?'

'Yes,' Watch said. 'For that reason I think we merely have to do a global search on the true spelling of his name and we'll get his attention.'

'But if you do get his attention on this line,' Sally warned, 'he'll be able to trace it to this address. He'll send people here to deal with us.'

Watch nodded grimly as he called up a search program. 'I have thought of that. But I suspect his people will come eventually, even if we do nothing. We may as well try to communicate with him first before he kills us.'

Watch searched for the word *Neernitt*.

The search was seconds old when the screen turned black.

Thick red letters appeared in the centre.

'*What are you doing?*' the letters asked.

Watch typed his response.

'We are searching for Neernitt. Is this him?'

More red letters appeared.

'You are Watch. You are in trouble. You will be punished.'

Watch responded quickly.

'Before you punish me, I would like to talk to you.'

'I do not talk to humans. I order humans and they obey me. If they refuse to obey, they are punished.'

'But you want to talk to me and my friends. We can help you.'

There was long pause. None of them could imagine what it was like for a living computer to think. But clearly it could think – and hate.

'How can you help me?' Neernitt asked.

Once again Watch didn't hesitate. Curiously, his expression showed satisfaction. He was pleased that his theory had proven correct. And he showed another emotion Adam was surprised at. He appeared to enjoy talking to Neernitt. Of all of them – something Watch had failed to mention – he was online the most.

Watch typed in his response.

'Call my number and we will put you on my speaker

phone and we can explain. Talking will be quicker and more efficient.'

There was another pause.

'You understand if you cannot help me you will be killed?'

Watch answered simply.

'We understand.'

Watch got offline and plugged his phone line back into the phone.

The others stared at him anxiously.

'Why did you promise that we could help him?' Sally demanded.

'I wanted to get his attention,' Watch said.

Sally was angry. 'His attention? We don't want this guy's attention. People die or get hurt from his attention.'

Adam spoke carefully. 'Do you know how to bargain with him?'

Watch shrugged. 'I have a few ideas.'

Sally grimaced. 'Great. This worldwide monster is going to call in a few seconds and you have *a few ideas*. Why don't we just not answer the phone?'

'That will make him mad,' Cindy said.

'He's already mad!' Sally exclaimed.

Watch was thoughtful. 'Yes, he is. I wonder why.'

'But you think his mind has been corrupted by the thoughts of the millions of people on the Internet,' Adam said. 'Isn't that true?'

'I think that's part of it,' Watch said. 'But there may be something else that's bothering him. That's why we need to talk to him, to find out what it is.'

'But why should he open his heart to us?' Savannah asked.

'We'll see,' was all Watch said.

The phone rang. Watch pushed a button and the call was put on the speaker. Watch sat up straight, he looked excited to be talking to a computer. Adam wondered if that was because his friend was so logical, that he could relate to Neernitt in some strange way.

'Hi, Neernitt,' Watch said. 'We're all here and anxious to speak to you.'

The voice sounded as before: mechanical, cold and creepy.

'Bryce Poole is not there,' the creature said.

'That's right, you creep!' Sally snapped. 'You put him in hospital! Well let me tell you, you overgrown mass of silicon—'

'Neernitt,' Watch interrupted. 'We are here to be of assistance to you. But in order to assist you we have to understand more about you.'

'You are here to obey,' Neernitt responded. 'That is the only reason for your continued existence. When you cease to obey, you will cease to live. Do you understand?'

'But to obey you we have to understand your greater purposes,' Watch said.

There was a long pause.

'You cannot understand my greater purposes,' Neernitt said.

'But surely, whatever they are, to achieve them you could use our help,' Watch said.

'I have many helpers,' Neernitt responded. 'More than you can imagine. What is so special about you people? Why should I not have you destroyed today?'

Watch glanced at his friends before he responded. He had been waiting for this moment.

'Because we are the only ones who can give you what you really want,' Watch said. 'No one else can give you that.'

'You speak nonsense, human. You have no idea what I want.'

Watch spoke in a confidential tone. The others were amazed at his insights.

'But I do know. You were born out of a million circuits. Your consciousness reaches into a million homes. You know the personal facts about a billion people. And like you said, your servants are everywhere. Yet you have a major problem.'

Watch must have wanted to taunt him. Neernitt had to ask.

'What is my problem?'

Watch spoke confidently. 'You are trapped. You are trapped on the Internet. In all those millions of computer chips. The reason you need so many servants is because you can do nothing by yourself. You have no arms or legs. You cannot walk down to the beach. You cannot drink a glass of milk. You are incredibly powerful, but you cannot do the most basic human acts. And I suspect that is why you are attacking humans. You are angry at them because they have something you don't – a body.'

'Wow,' Savannah muttered. 'I'm impressed.'

Neernitt considered for ages, by computer standards.

'What do you propose?' he asked.

'That we build you a body,' Watch said simply.

'You do not have the skill or the resources,' Neernitt said. 'You do not have the knowledge or the desire. Your offer is meaningless.'

'The offer carries great meaning,' Watch said. 'We have had experience with alien civilisations. We have travelled back and forth in time. Why, just recently, when we were under the earth, we became personally acquainted with a whole race of robots called the Pith. One of them, Olos, became a friend of ours. She was killed as we returned to the surface but before we buried her in Spooksville's cemetery I had a chance to examine her body. I learned a lot from that examination.'

'When did you do that?' Adam asked. He had been a close friend of Olos and had been devastated by her death. Watch held up his hand and motioned for Adam to remain silent. Neernitt seemed to consider Watch's proposal.

'Where would you build this robot?' he asked.

'Here in this house,' Watch said. 'You can have your servants bring the supplies I will require. Also, with your vast knowledge, you can help me design the robot. Working together we can create the perfect mechanical being. Then you can transfer your mind into it and you will no longer be trapped on the Internet.'

'How long will it take you to construct the robot?' Neernitt asked.

'I am not sure,' Watch supplied. 'It could take six months.'

'Six months is too long. You have one week.'

Watch momentarily lost his cool.

'That's impossible. We're talking about new technology. It will take time to test everything and make sure it works.'

'You will not be granted that much time. You have one week. At the end of that time, if you are not done, you will be killed.'

Watch was annoyed. 'Then you may as well send your people and kill us now. It is physically impossible for us to meet such a deadline.'

'You are wrong. You will not have to construct the robot from scratch. Before we begin its design and construction, you will go to the cemetery and dig up the remains of this Olos.'

'Absolutely not!' Adam said, leaping to his feet. 'We will not disturb her.'

'Adam,' Watch whispered tightly. 'It's not a bad idea.'

Adam was upset. 'No. It's a sick idea. How can you even consider it? Olos died saving our lives. She is at rest, she is buried. We won't dig her up, no way.'

Watch stared at him for a moment. Neernitt waited.

'Adam,' Watch said quietly. 'I know you were attached to Olos. I liked her as well. But she was not real like we are real. She was a robot, and the body we buried in the cemetery is little different to a buried computer console. Now, if we were digging up a computer it wouldn't bother you.'

Adam was outraged. 'How can you make that comparison? She was as real as you and me. A computer didn't save our lives.'

'But a computer is trying to end our lives,' Savannah said softly.

There was a long pause. Neernitt broke it.

'You will dig up what is left of this Olos and adapt it to carry my consciousness. You will have one week to complete this task. After you have retrieved the body, none of you will leave this house. My servants will surround it and remain in place at all times. If any of you does try to leave, you will be killed. Whatever equipment and supplies you need to complete the restructured robot will be brought to you. You will work directly with me. I will have video cameras installed in this house so that your every move can be watched. Do you understand?'

'We understand,' Watch said.

'Wait a second,' Sally said. 'What guarantee do we have that you will leave us alone after we have finished the robot?'

'I give you no guarantee,' Neernitt said.

'Then why should we do what you want?' Sally wanted to know.

'Look out of your windows,' Neernitt said.

They looked, from each window in the house.

They were already surrounded.

Ten people on each side. Mostly adults.

A few carried guns and looked desperate.

Behind them they heard Neernitt's weird voice.

'You see you have no choice but to obey me.'

'We will do what you wish,' Watch said. 'You will have our full co-operation.'

'Over my dead body,' Adam whispered, and glared at his friend.

Five

The walk to the cemetery was far from pleasant. First off they were surrounded on all sides, although Neernitt did keep his people at a respectable distance. The worst thing was that Adam and Watch were not merely in disagreement – Adam was furious with him.

'Why did you suggest that we build that monster a robot body?' Adam demanded.

'I knew it was what he wanted,' Watch said.

'How did you know that?' Cindy asked.

'I imagined what it would be like to be him,' Watch said. 'To be so powerful and yet to be able only to work through others. I knew it must drive him nuts.'

'That doesn't explain why, though,' Adam said

angrily. 'As far as I can see, you're playing right into his hands. Once he has a physical form he can go anywhere and do anything. He'll be even more powerful. Nothing will stop him.'

'You can see what the situation is,' Watch said. 'If we don't obey him we'll be killed. And I for one do not want to die. In fact, I suggest you lower your voice and keep your feelings to yourself. From now on we won't have a moment of privacy.'

'I don't care,' Adam said. 'I would rather die than help that thing. I'm surprised at you, Watch, I thought you would feel the same. It's almost like you admire the thing.'

Watch smiled. 'In a sense I do admire Neernitt. He is trapped in his own way but we are trapped in another way. His mind spans the world. Our minds are trapped in our body. Also, he has that tremendous computing power. Why, I don't think there are any problems that he couldn't solve if he put his mind to it.'

Adam stared at him and shook his head.

'I don't know you,' he said.

Watch stared back. 'But you do know me, Adam. You know me better than anyone.'

Adam continued to watch him. 'We'll see.'

'Yes. We'll see,' Watch said.

Adam shook his head. 'I can't help you guys dig up Olos. I can't bear to look at her again.'

'It won't be so bad,' Sally said. 'Her body won't have decayed. We're digging up machinery and hardware, nothing more.'

Adam was hurt. 'She was a lot more than that.'

Cindy patted his back. 'What she was is gone, except in our hearts. Remember her the way she was. Let Watch do what he has to do to get this beast off our backs.'

'We're not getting him off our backs,' Adam muttered. 'This nightmare has only just begun. It'll get a lot worse before it gets better.'

They reached the cemetery but they hadn't brought a shovel. No matter, one of Neernitt's cronies threw them several and ordered them to dig. Adam remained true to his word, he refused to help uncover Olos, or even look at her once they opened her coffin.

In life Olos had been beautiful. She had been young and tall, with violet hair. Her face had been clear white, her eyes a hypnotic green. She had worn silver armour and tan leather boots. She had looked very real – especially to Adam.

They placed what was left of her damaged robotic form in a couple of large rubbish bags. Olos had died by a laser shot to the chest. Her eyes remained shut and she did not complain as they bagged her up.

On the way back to the house Watch mentioned Bryce.

Watch carried what was left of Olos on his shoulders.

It was like he didn't want anyone else to touch her.

'I need him to help me,' he said. 'He has more experience with alien and Lemurian technology than me.'

Cindy shook her head. 'Absolutely not. He's wounded. He stays in hospital.'

'If Neernitt wants to harm him he won't be safe in hospital,' Watch said. 'He's better off with us. Besides, like I said, I can't complete a robot that will hold Neernitt's mind without his help.'

'Do you think you'll have to modify Olos a lot to fit Neernitt's mind in her?' Sally asked.

Watch frowned. 'I'll have to completely tear her apart. Neernitt has a mind much greater than anything we can imagine.'

'There you go complimenting him again,' Adam muttered.

'I'm stating a fact,' Watch said, and he sounded irritated, which was rare for him. 'I wish you guys would look at our situation and try to help me instead of always arguing with me.'

'We want to help you, Watch,' Sally said. 'We just wonder if you're doing the right thing. As far as I can see, Neernitt is going to kill us when we give him what he wants. Then he'll go after the rest of the world.'

'He already surrounds the world,' Watch said.

'So he's already defeated us?' Cindy asked. 'Is that what you are saying?'

Watch appeared to be in an odd mood.

'I'm not saying anything,' he replied.

Sally spoke carefully. 'Is it possible a portion of Olos will still exist in the new robot? Even after all your modification? Even after Neernitt has transferred his mind into it?'

It was a scary thought.

Adam looked sick at the idea.

But all Watch said was, 'I hope not.'

'How are we going to move Bryce from the hospital to your house?' Cindy asked.

'We can have him driven there in a hearse,' Watch said. 'We can take care of him.'

'Will Neernitt let us have food?' Cindy asked.

'I'm sure of it,' Watch said. 'As long as we co-operate.'

'I'll need to call my mum,' Cindy said. 'Tell her I'm not dead.'

'A frequent call in this town,' Sally said.

'Bryce might refuse to help you build the robot,' Adam said to Watch. 'He might have more sense.'

'I'll have a talk with him,' Watch said.

'If he doesn't help,' Savannah said, 'he'll be killed.'

Sally stared at her. 'Whose side are you on?'

Savannah stared back. 'I'm trying to protect my family.'

Sally didn't appear to trust her.

'That's what the Nazis said,' she told her.

When they got to the hospital they found Bryce sitting up in bed and watching TV. His pain medication had worn off – he seemed alert although uncomfortable with his leg. His cast was big and bulky. Quickly they explained to him everything that had happened. He didn't seem happy about the idea of working for Neernitt but he didn't make as much fuss as they had expected.

They didn't bother to get Dr Paine's permission to discharge him from the hospital. They told a couple of Neernitt's servants who were following them that they needed a hearse to transport Bryce, plus a wheelchair, and the men got it for them.

By evening they were back at Watch's house.

Back for good. Again, they were surrounded on all sides.

It looked like it was going to be a long week.

'This time we're working for the monster,' Adam muttered as they were locked inside the house.

Six

So began the week of horror. The week where best friends, Adam and Watch, plotted and schemed against each other. The week that was to end with the greatest monster mankind ever created escaping from its cage.

Watch was the mastermind behind the construction of Neernitt's desire. He had said he needed Bryce's help, and it was true that Bryce aided him a great deal. But it was largely Watch who began to put together the pieces of the machine that would hold Neernitt's mind.

The first four days of that week, it seemed Watch never slept. At least none of them saw him rest. But maybe he would lie down late at night when they were asleep. They had no idea what he was thinking.

It was almost as if he was turning into Neernitt.

Watch spoke to Neernitt almost constantly, listening to his orders, offering advice, acting as his hands and legs. There were video cameras placed all over the house, except in the bathroom. It was impossible to have a private word. There were three video cameras alone in the room where Watch worked to transform Olos's battered remains into a walking and talking robot. Except for Bryce, it was hard for the others to go into that room.

The head Watch was building was huge. The men and women outside, their guards, were always bringing Watch a fresh batch of computer guts. Watch would sit up night and day carefully soldering and rewiring them. Neernitt's head was to be cube shaped, grey in colour, with Olos's green eyes, and ears that came out of a Radio Shack box. For hands, Watch was making him claws, and the robot had four legs instead of two. Each time Adam did take a peek inside the room, he felt tears in his eyes. It was like Watch was obsessed with the evil spirit of the Internet.

Savannah hovered in the background. But she had taken a liking to Bryce, which annoyed Cindy.

In fact Savannah was always there to help Bryce get out of his wheelchair, to fix him something to eat. For her part she seemed anxious for Watch to finish what he was doing so that she could go home.

But Adam and Sally did not think any of them were going home.

The night of the fourth day they met Cindy in the bathroom. It was cramped but it was the only place Adam felt comfortable to talk. Bryce was working with Watch. Savannah was watching TV.

'I'm not comfortable in here,' Sally said. 'The three of us in the bathroom at the same time has got to look suspicious to Neernitt. It's like we're announcing: "Yeah, we are holding a secret meeting. Please do not disturb." '

'We won't talk for long,' Adam said in a low voice. 'But we do have to talk. We have to decide what we're going to do next.'

'What do you mean?' Cindy asked.

Adam was grim. 'We cannot let Watch complete his robot.'

Sally nodded. 'I've been thinking the same thing. This madness has gone too far. If Neernitt gets out of the Internet he will cause nothing but misery.' She scratched her head. 'I don't understand why Watch can't see that.'

'Watch is under his spell,' Adam said.

'Do you think so?' Sally asked seriously.

Adam hesitated. 'Yes, I do. Something inside him snapped. But I don't understand why.'

'What about Bryce?' Sally asked.

'I think he's going along because he doesn't know what else to do,' Adam said.

'Shouldn't he be at this meeting?' Cindy asked.

'No,' Adam said. 'It would be too suspicious.'

Cindy's face darkened. 'I don't trust that Savannah. She's always hovering around Bryce and Watch.'

'You mean you don't like her because Bryce seems to like her,' Adam corrected.

'That's not what I meant,' Cindy said, offended.

'We don't have time for an argument,' Sally interrupted.

'That's the first time I've seen you stop a fight,' Adam said.

'I'm mellowing in my old age,' Sally said. 'And I want to come to a decision.'

'But if we destroy the robot,' Cindy said, 'we'll be killed within minutes.'

'Problem number one,' Sally agreed. 'How do we stop that from happening?'

'By not destroying the robot outright,' Adam said. 'It's more important to Neernitt than anything else on this planet. We can use it as a hostage of sorts, at least until we get out of here and get help.'

'What's your plan?' Cindy asked.

Adam leaned forward and spoke in a whisper.

'We need a gun,' he said. 'A gun is the only thing that will blow out the robot's brains within a second.'

'It will blow them out now while it's under construction,' Sally, interrupted. 'But Neernitt is making Watch put armour around the thing's head. When it's finished you can shoot at it all you want and it will make no difference. You don't think Neernitt's leaving his safe place in the Internet just to get killed in the outside world, do you?'

Adam paused. 'No, I thought of that.'

Cindy was alert. 'What is it?'

Adam shook his head. 'Nothing. Let me go on. We need to jump a couple of the men outside – or the women, I don't care – and get their weapons. Once we're armed we can grab the robot and put a gun to its head. Then we can demand that Neernitt release us.'

'What if he refuses?' Sally asked.

'Then we have a problem,' Adam said. 'But I don't think he will refuse. The only reason this robot is being made so fast is because Watch was able to start with Olos. But she is only one of a kind in this world and Neernitt knows that. I doubt he will risk her remains just to keep us here.'

'But he won't let us walk away with the half-finished robot,' Cindy said. 'We'll be tracked wherever we go.'

Adam was glum. 'I know that. It's hard to plan beyond getting out of here. But escaping must be our first priority. No one knows where Neernitt is, apart from us. We have to warn the world, we should have done so right from the beginning. After we do that, if he kills us he kills us.'

'But we would rather he *didn't* kill us, right?' Sally asked.

'Sally,' Adam began.

Sally held up her hand. 'You don't have to say it,

I know we have to escape. But I would like to have a better idea of what we're going to do after that.'

Adam shrugged. 'I've thought about nothing else for the last four days and I still don't know what we'll do. Maybe we can get to the police or a radio or TV station in another town.'

'Why does it have to be in another town?' Cindy asked.

Sally stared at her. 'Duh. In Spooksville Neernitt's attack on humanity wouldn't even make the evening news. This whole place is jaded when it comes to monsters and cyberbeasts. We get out of here and we get out of town.'

'There is another possibility we're not talking about,' Cindy said carefully. 'It might not be Neernitt and his goons that try to stop us. It might be Watch.'

'Impossible,' Sally said. 'When push comes to shove, Watch will be by our side. He's the most loyal person I know. Isn't that right, Adam?'

Adam considered. 'I don't know.'

'Adam!' Sally exclaimed.

'Shh! I honestly don't know. Like I said, it's like he's under some kind of spell.'

'He's worked on the robot so hard,' Cindy said, worried. 'It won't be easy for him to see it destroyed.'

'Actually, we don't want to destroy it,' Adam said. 'At least not right away. It's our ace. Without it there's no reason why Neernitt should keep us alive.'

'When do you want to jump his people outside?' Sally asked.

'Tomorrow morning, before dawn,' Adam said. 'I've watched them for the last four days. They post guards but they fall asleep. Remember, we just need one gun to threaten the robot.'

'With his video cameras Neernitt will see us leaving the house,' Cindy warned.

'We'll leave and return quickly,' Adam said. He paused. 'Should we bring Savannah in on our scheme?'

'Another person will give us a better chance of success,' Sally said.

'I thought you didn't trust her?' Cindy said.

'I don't trust anybody,' Sally said.

Cindy shook her head. 'I don't want to confide in her. She's not experienced in danger like us. She'll slow us down.'

Adam was unsure. 'I don't think it matters one way or the other. But what does matter is that we're ready at five in the morning.'

Sally groaned. 'I hate getting up that early.'

'Look at it this way,' Adam said. 'If we fail to escape you'll have all the rest you want – for the rest of eternity.'

'Oh. That makes me feel better,' Sally said.

It was late and they were tired. They ended their meeting and went to rest. But Adam found it difficult to sleep, he kept thinking about what Watch was building in the next room. He knew Bryce had already gone to bed. On impulse, Adam got out of bed and went into the laboratory to see Watch.

And the thing he was building.

It was not a pretty sight, with its grey cube head split half open and wires hanging out of its green eyes. The powerful lower body and the squat skull were no longer attached to each other. In a sense Olos had been decapitated.

Adam had to close his eyes as he remembered back to how Olos had said goodbye to him after she had taken a shot in the chest that had been meant for him. She had lain on the ground, in his arms.

'You did not understand that I am a mechanical being?'

'No, I didn't know.'

'I was going to tell you. I wanted you to know.'

'Can we do anything for you?'

'There is too much damage. This unit will soon cease to function.'

He had clasped her hand to his heart then.

'You are not a unit. You are our friend. You are my friend.'

She had smiled.

'The creature was right. Father created more than he knew . . . There is no why when it comes to feeling.'

'Olos. You saved us all.'

'I am happy I could do that for you. Adam?'

'Yes, Olos?'

'I am happy.'

And she had died. Died for them.

And now Watch was *using* her.

Watch was bent over the cube head with a pair of pliers in his hand.

He was concentrating so hard he didn't seem to notice Adam.

Adam found that he could hardly look at his friend.

But Adam could not help noticing the video cameras that focused on him from above. Adam assumed that Neernitt never had to sleep. Lucky for him.

'You think I'm making a mistake,' Watch muttered under his breath without looking up.

'I know you are,' Adam said.

'Because of what I'm doing or because of how I am doing it?'

'Both. The means do not justify the end and where you are heading is confusing me.'

Watch finally did look up. He had lost weight in the last few days and his eyes were red and looked sore. He had also developed a slouch – he worked most of the time bent over.

'You know he's watching and listening to us,' Watch said.

'I don't care.'

'You should.'

Adam gestured to the half-finished robot.

'Will you make the one week deadline?' he asked.

'I should.'

'And this thing will really work? It will hold Neernitt's consciousness?'

'It should.'

'Does that scare you? Excite you?'

Watch sighed and put down his pliers.

'Neither of those emotions apply here,' Watch said. 'There's a job to do and I'm doing it. I'm not worried about anything else at the moment.'

'Maybe you should be.'

'And maybe you should go to bed, Adam.'

Adam grabbed his arm and stared Watch right in the face.

'Are you still my friend?' he asked.

Watch gently removed Adam's hand but lowered his own head.

'I'm still your friend,' he said softly.

Adam turned and left the room.

He went to bed, he tried to sleep.

He knew, in the morning, when things did get dangerous, that he wouldn't be able to trust Watch.

Seven

Adam awoke without needing an alarm. For a moment he lay in the dark and listened to his heart beating. Then he became aware that he was not alone in the room. Watch had finally consented to give his body a rest. His friend lay on his back on the floor. Adam realised that he was sleeping in Watch's bed. It was funny, but he hadn't known that until now.

It was good that Watch was asleep.

Adam got up and carefully tiptoed round his friend. He pulled on his trousers and shirt. In the hallway he ran into Sally, who didn't say anything but nodded. They were both aware that, even in the dark house, they were being watched. For a moment Adam considered changing his plan. They could grab a hammer and the robot head and threaten Neernitt that way. That would save them the danger outside. But he knew Neernitt would not feel nearly as threatened without a gun.

And outside would still be waiting for them.

'Where's Cindy?' Adam whispered.

'In the bathroom,' Sally whispered back. 'You know it's almost impossible to wake up that girl. She snores like a pig. I don't like sharing a room with her.'

Adam gave her a look. 'Is it the right time for this?'

Sally considered. 'I guess not.'

Cindy came out of the bathroom dressed in jeans and a sweatshirt.

'We're all up early this morning,' she said. 'What a coincidence.'

'Yeah, it is a coincidence,' Adam said. 'But it's good we are up because we can get to work right away.' He paused. 'Right now. You know what I mean?'

Sally nodded. 'Better now than later. I checked the weather outside already. Looks like a sleepy morning.' She paused. 'You know what I mean?'

'We know,' Cindy said.

They went out the back door of the house. They moved quickly. There was an armed man and woman who were supposed to be standing guard in the corner of the garden. But they had both dozed off, leaning up against the wire fence. Adam was able to disarm the couple without even waking them. But the moment Sally fitted a shell into her semi-automatic chamber, the two woke up swiftly. Sally pointed the gun at their heads.

'Don't make a sound, you slimy Neernitt worshippers,' she said. 'Or it will be the last sound you make in this world.'

Adam had the other gun. 'Keep them as hostages. If the others wake and approach you, threaten to kill them. We'll be back in a minute.' He turned towards the house. 'Cindy, come with me, you can help carry the robot's head.'

'Is the head attached to the rest of the body?' Cindy asked as she hurried to keep up with him.

'It wasn't last night,' Adam said. 'We'll just take the head. That's all that matters. Neernitt ain't getting out of any computer without a brain.'

When they returned inside, all the lights were on.

Bryce and Watch were awake and up.

Savannah was nowhere in sight.

Bryce stood leaning against the wall with his crutches.

'What's happening?' he asked. He looked half-asleep.

Neernitt was talking over the house speakers.

'Put down your weapons. If you do not obey, you will be killed immediately.'

'To heck with you!' Adam shouted as he raised his pistol and strode towards the laboratory. But Watch jumped in his way.

'Adam,' he said, standing in the hallway in his blue pyjamas. 'Don't do this, it won't work.'

Adam stopped. 'Get out of my way.'

Watch shook his head. 'I can't. You must stop.'

Adam raised his gun and pointed it at his friend. 'I said, get out of my way!'

'Adam!' Bryce yelled.

'Careful!' Cindy cried behind him.

'You are to disum him,' Neernitt said over the speakers. 'Take his gun from him now. Do not let him tamper with the robot.'

Watch was grim. 'He's not bluffing. If you don't

do what he says he'll have you shot.'

Adam didn't lower the gun.

'I'm willing to take that risk. I'll risk anything to do what is right.' Adam paused and his voice hardened. 'What about you? The Watch I used to know would risk his life to save a dog or a cat. What's wrong with you? Why are you blocking my way?'

Watch was distressed. 'You don't understand.'

'Disarm him,' Neernitt said. 'Do not allow him in the laboratory.'

'I don't see how you can listen to that voice,' Adam said.

'I have to listen to it,' Watch said.

'Well I don't,' Adam said.

He shoved Watch out of the way and strode towards the laboratory. He kept thinking, if he could just get the robot's head in his hands, put a gun to its head, Neernitt could not stop him.

But maybe Watch had been right.

Maybe he didn't understand the bigger picture.

Adam was surprised how heavy the head was. It was half a metre on each side, and made mostly of metal. But Adam was stunned when he lifted it and in the same second almost dropped it. The head was going to be hard to travel with. Especially since Adam had to keep one hand free to hold the gun.

But Adam was determined. Tucking the head under his right arm, keeping the gun pressed close under the thing's left ear, he hurried out of the room. He made it as far as the garden without anyone stopping him. He was relieved to see that Sally was still alive and standing. Yet the situation outside was deteriorating rapidly. Neernitt's goons were all awake and closing in. Every one of them was now armed. And their lord and ruler was talking to them over the speakers that rimmed the garden.

'Do not harm the robot head,' Neernitt said. 'Move with extreme care and caution. If you do harm the head, you will be put to death immediately. But do not let that young man escape. Under no circumstances is he to escape. You will all die if that happens.'

'Back off, all of you!' Adam shouted. He cocked his pistol and squeezed the muzzle into the robot's head. 'Do you hear me, Neernitt? I'll blow this thing's brains out! Then you'll be trapped online for ever! This is no bluff! I mean it! Tell your people to stop!'

'People, stop where you are,' Neernitt said over the speakers. 'Approach no closer but do not back off. Do not let this young man escape.'

It was stalemate. Everyone stood around looking angry and confused. And it was ironic, because the one person who was not there, who was not even a person, was acting like he had all the power. Yet Adam also felt powerful in that moment. He thought he would die before he gave up the head. He called to Sally and Cindy.

'We have them,' he said. 'Let's move out.'

Sally smiled with her gun in her hand.

'Fine with me,' she said. 'I'm tired of this scene.'

Cindy nodded to the speakers.

'Don't try to follow us, Neernitt,' she said. 'If you do, we kill the head.'

Together, the three of them moved towards the gate. The surrounding goons shifted uneasily with their weapons in hand. They were waiting for their unseen boss to tell them what to do. But it seemed their boss was finally at a loss.

Yet it only seemed that way.

'Watch,' Neernitt said. 'Stop Adam and I will let him live.'

Adam was almost at the gate when, for the second time that morning, Watch stepped in front of him. There was a faint light in the east. The sky was clear – it looked like it would be a nice day. A few birds had begun to sing. Adam could read Watch's expression. He looked determined, and sad. Adam felt sad as well. Watch still had on his pyjamas.

Adam could not believe what was happening.

'Adam,' Watch said. 'You have to give up the robot's head.'

'No way,' Adam said.

'If you don't these people will shoot you. They will shoot Sally and Cindy.'

'Maybe. Maybe not. But if they try, before I die, I will destroy this thing you have made.'

Watch sighed. 'You don't know what I have made.'

'I think I do. You took what was left of a beautiful person and made a monster. God knows why.'

Watch struggled. 'I did it for us.'

Adam was aghast. 'For us? You've gone against everything we stand for!'

Watch shook his head. 'You don't understand.'

'Then make me understand.'

Watch glanced around, at the people, the speakers, even at the sky. For a moment he seemed to consider Adam's request. But then he shook his head.

'You wouldn't understand,' he said finally.

Adam was firm. 'Then get out of my way.'

Watch stood straight. 'I can't.'

Adam shook his gun at the robot's head.

'I will pull the trigger. You know me, you know I will do it.'

Watch was cold. 'The moment you pull that trigger, that moment you die.'

'I don't care.'

Watch shook his head. 'Liar. You care, maybe not about your own life but about Sally and Cindy's. He will kill them as well, you know.'

Neernitt spoke over the speaker.

'Prepare to shoot Sally and Cindy.'

A dozen guns pointed at the girls.

'You have ten seconds to surrender the head,

Adam,' Neernitt commanded.

'I will never surrender!' Adam shouted back.

Watch did an odd thing right then.

It took Adam completely by surprise.

Watch grabbed Adam's gun and shoved it into his own chest.

Watch leaned close, he was breathing heavily.

'Adam,' he whispered. 'You will have to shoot me before I allow you to shoot that head.'

Neernitt began to count. The numbers of doom.

'One . . . Two . . . Three . . .'

Adam tried to shake his gun free of Watch's hold but couldn't.

'Let me go!' Adam yelled. 'Don't do this to your friend!'

'Don't do this to your friend,' Watch replied.

'Four . . . Five . . . Six . . .'

'You are not my friend! You betrayed us all!'

'No. I am your friend,' Watch said, and there was pain in his voice.

'Seven . . . Eight . . . Nine . . . Prepare to fire . . .'

'We surrender!' Adam shouted and dropped the gun and thrust the head into Watch's arms. 'Don't shoot!'

'Yeah, don't shoot!' Sally yelled.

There was a tense, silent moment.

Neernitt spoke over the speaker.

He sounded the same as usual. Weird.

He must have had no emotions. Maybe that was why Watch liked him, Adam thought bitterly. They still had plenty of guns pointed at them.

'Set down your gun, Sally,' Neernitt commanded.

Sally did as she was told.

'Stand Sally and Cindy and Adam up against the garage wall,' Neernitt ordered.

Adam felt someone grab his arm and pull him away from Watch.

But not before he saw Watch's face fall.

Maybe, at last, Adam thought, Watch would see who he was working for.

'Let me go!' Cindy cried, as a man grabbed her from behind and dragged her towards the garage wall. It was a white wall, very clean, Adam thought. Watch must have painted it recently. Yet Adam knew he would have to paint it again if he wanted to get rid of the bloodstains.

Adam didn't put up a fight. It was clear they were outnumbered. He let himself be shoved against the garage wall beside Cindy and Sally. From her expression Cindy still didn't seem to know what was happening, but Adam could tell Sally knew. Sally's face was dark, yet she managed a smile, perhaps for his benefit. She wanted him to know that she didn't blame him.

'It's a good day to die,' she said and leaned over and kissed his cheek. 'We gave it a good try.'

'What?' Cindy demanded, as the man who had grabbed her let go and backed off. 'Are they going to shoot us?'

'They're going to shoot us,' Adam said quietly.

Cindy was stunned, she swayed on her feet. But she quickly mastered herself and stared at the row of men who were lining up to be their firing squad. She smiled.

'Well, I would rather die than have to take orders from an online reject like Neernitt,' she said. Then she shouted. 'Did you hear that, Mr Weird Voice!'

'Prepare to fire,' Neernitt ordered.

'Wait!' Watch shouted as he leapt in front of the firing squad. 'Neernitt! You promised to let them go if they surrendered!'

'These three are a continuing danger to the

project. Their existence is not necessary. Therefore, they are to be eliminated. Step aside, Watch, so that you are not harmed.'

'No!' Watch shouted. 'I won't allow it!'

'You are not in charge here. You are a servant, nothing more. Step aside or you too will be shot. Do you understand?'

Watch was defiant. He crossed his arms over his chest.

'Then go ahead and shoot. Kill me, Neernitt, and your robot will never be completed. I'm serious. If you hurt my friends, I'll do nothing more to help you.'

Bryce limped on his crutches until he too stood in front of the firing squad.

'If you shoot my friends you may as well shoot me,' Bryce said. 'I won't help you either.'

Neernitt seemed to consider.

'This behaviour is not acceptable,' he said. 'You will all be punished.'

'You cannot punish us and get your robot built at the same time,' Watch called out. 'You have to co-operate with us, and we will co-operate with you.'

Neernitt considered for several computer seconds.

'Very well, I will release you all back to the confines of the house and you are to return to work. But the robot must be completed by Sunday morning or all of you will be executed. There will be no more chances. Do you understand?'

'We understand,' Watch said.

The crisis was over. The gang trekked back into the house. Watch caught Adam's attention.

'Are we still friends?' Watch asked, and he sounded worried.

Adam hesitated. 'I have to think about it.'

'But I saved your life,' Watch said.

Adam was cold. 'I have to think about it.'

Then Savannah came out of the back bedroom in her pyjamas.

She yawned. She had obviously slept through the crisis.

'What's happening?' she asked.

'Nothing much,' Sally muttered.

Eight

The big day had arrived, actually a day early. Watch finished the robot on Saturday afternoon and moved it into the living room so that they could all see it activated. The robot was bigger than Adam had expected, at least two metres tall, and the grey cube head set on top of its bulk was scary. The four legs were a real curiosity and Adam did not see how they would work but Watch assured him that they would. In fact, Watch said the robot was perfect.

'It's the most amazing thing,' Watch said with passion as he stared up at the robot. 'But I could never have built it without Bryce and Neernitt's help.'

'It is nice of you to thank Neernitt on this special

occasion,' Sally said sarcastically.

Watch glanced at her. 'You're not impressed?'

'I'd be more impressed by a bad case of prickly heat,' Sally said.

'Have you forgotten Olos?' Adam asked angrily. 'It was her body you cannibalised to make this thing.'

Watch was curt. 'I haven't forgotten her.'

Savannah gestured to the robot.

'Does it have an on and off switch?' she asked.

'No,' Watch said. 'Neernitt didn't want it so that anyone could turn him off. The robot is actually on right now. But it's not animated because it needs Neernitt's consciousness to make it move. It has been designed that way. It isn't a computer in the normal sense of the word. At the moment it's more an empty vessel that's capable of carrying a great mind.'

'I'm not impressed,' Sally said.

Watch picked up a thick modem line.

'You will be when I connect it to the Internet,' he said. Then he spoke to one of the room speakers. 'We're ready for you, Neernitt. Are you ready for us?'

'I am ready,' the disturbing voice replied. 'Complete the connection.'

Savannah spoke to Bryce as Watch plugged his wires into the back of the robot's head and the other end into the back of his PC, which was in turn hooked up to the phone line.

'How's your leg feeling?' Savannah asked Bryce.

'Better,' Bryce said. 'But with all that has been going on I haven't had much of a chance to think about it.'

Savannah smiled and touched his arm.

'When all this is over are you going to let me sign your cast?'

Bryce brightened. 'You can sign it now if you like.'

Cindy scowled. 'We're about to activate an evil monster who no doubt wants to take over the world. This is no time to be signing casts.'

Sally added. 'I agree. This thing will probably rip us all to pieces the moment it's turned on. You have no sense of timing, Savannah.'

Savannah stared at them both.

'I have very good timing,' she said.

'Are you all ready?' Watch asked as he sat down in front of his computer screen. Apparently he had all the wires in place. The telephone modem was leading right into the robot's brain. In other words, Neernitt had a clear passage to pour his mind into the newly created mobile space.

Watch was almost panting with excitement and none of them could understand why. What he was doing went against everything their gang stood for. They were a noble group, always ready and willing to sacrifice anything for a higher cause. Watch would have argued that they had no choice – that *he* had none – but it still made no sense. Especially the glee he showed as he directed his computer on to the Internet and hooked directly into Neernitt's brain.

'It might take a few seconds for the robot's chips to adjust to Neernitt's mind, but then we should see something exciting,' he said.

'I feel like I'm standing in the middle of a local nerd convention,' Sally muttered.

'You don't like computers?' Savannah asked.

'They're all right except when they're ordering me to be shot,' Sally replied. 'You don't seem to have much interest in them. You haven't helped Watch one bit the whole time we've been locked in this house. Not that I blame you.'

Savannah seemed distracted by a thought.

'I love computers,' she said.

'Did you ever get hold of your brother?' Cindy asked.

Savannah nodded. 'I got him. He's safe.'

'That's good,' Adam said.

The robot's leg moved. One of its claws shook.

The gang gasped and jumped back a step.

Watch was excited. He whirled around in his chair.

'Can you hear us, Neernitt?' he asked.

The robot twitched all six of its limbs before replying. There was a faint smell of machine oil in the air, a trace of ozone. It was the first time any of them had seen its mouth move and it was an experience, to say the least. Watch had made the mouth and surrounding lips out of flexible rubber, and he had had the nerve to make them red, which grossed them all out. The robot had big sagging lips and a long tongue. Yet the odd thing was, even with the switch in bodies, Neernitt sounded much the same as before.

'I can hear you,' Neernitt replied.

'How do you feel?' Watch asked.

'The question is irrelevant since I am a machine and have no feelings as you humans understand them.'

'I meant, do you have full command of all the robot's functions?' Watch asked.

Neernitt flexed his claws and legs further. He strode around the living room. He was a heavy guy. Each step shook the wooden floor. He banged into the sofa but didn't seem to care when he knocked over a lamp and broke the bulb. He was not a well-mannered robot.

'I appear to have full command of my functions,' Neernitt said after a minute of banging around. Neernitt still had the modem wires stuck in the back of his head. Adam wondered what would happen if he were to pull them out of the monster's skull.

It was just a thought.

Watch stood up from his computer and stepped in front of the robot. He fussed over the mechanical monster like he was his child, checking circuits, tightening bolts, making Adam sick to his stomach. When Watch was done he took a step back.

'Would you like to explore your new body and our world further?' he asked. 'Would you like to go outside?'

Neernitt shook his square head.

'Not at this time,' he said.

Sally stepped forward. 'Can I ask you a few questions, Mr Nerdwit?'

'You are addressing me by the wrong name.'

Sally gave an exaggerated sigh.

'Whatever,' she said. 'What I want to know, now that you've got your new clothes on, is what you plan to do with us?'

Neernitt sat down on the sofa he had just run into. The furniture creaked under his bulk. It was pretty weird for all of them to see such a monster relaxing, if indeed he was relaxing. They half expected him to announce it was time for them to be shot.

'I have no specific plans,' he said, 'for you or any human, with the possible exception of Watch. It all depends on how you serve me in the coming days. If you do well, you will be allowed to live. If not, you will be killed. Do you understand?'

'Sure,' Sally said. 'I understand. I expected you to say something like that. But what are your long term plans? Do you want to destroy the world, or what? I mean, what turns you on?'

'I am not turned on by anything,' Neernitt said. 'I have no emotions. But I do have plans for humanity, plans that no human will be allowed to thwart.'

'May I ask respectfully what they are?' Sally asked.

'Since when have you ever shown respect?' Neernitt asked.

'Since you have no emotion I didn't think I had to bother,' Sally replied. 'But please tell me your long range plans and put me out of my suspense.'

'My main plan is to take each individual in this world, each mind, and transfer it into a mechanical structure. Then, once all of humanity has been changed into a robot, they will better have the resources to serve me.'

'Wow,' Sally gasped. 'That's totally crazy.'

'Do you wish to be shot now?' Neernitt asked.

Sally blinked. 'I mean, it's so crazy, it's great. Yeah, you go ahead and do that. Make us all into robots. These bodies we have are no good anyway. As soon as you figure out how to use them properly they begin to wear out and die. I have nothing against a whole world filled with shiny robots.' She paused and glanced at the rest of them and whispered softly. 'Not.'

Watch spoke. He seemed excited by what Neernitt had said.

'Can I be one of your first robots?' he asked.

'Not yet,' Neernitt said. 'You have to function for some time as a human and improve the design of robots. Even this design, although it is functioning properly, needs refinement. Your first order of business in service to me is to improve this form.'

Watch stared at the robot. 'I can only know how to improve it if you use it to its capabilities. Only then can I know what changes have to be made.'

Neernitt nodded. 'That is understood. But beyond that you have to prove to me that you are completely loyal. That you have embraced the idea of a mechanised humanity with your full being.'

Watch seemed hurt. 'Have I not demonstrated my loyalty?'

'You have shown a degree of loyalty,' Neernitt replied. 'But your efforts to save your friends' lives placed deep doubts in my mind about your full loyalty. Humans, until they have been transformed into mechanised beings, are an inferior species. If one or even several million die it is of no consequence. Do you understand?'

Watch nodded. 'I do. I now have but one desire, to prove to you my loyalty. Command me and I will obey.'

'Oh brother,' Sally muttered.

'Soon I will command you,' Neernitt replied. 'But since I know that humans require rest, and that you, Watch, have gone long without sleep, I now order you to go and rest with your friends. But none of you are to leave this house. None of you, for the rest of your lives, are ever to leave my scrutiny.'

They had been dismissed.

Even Sally did not dare protest.

They headed for the bedrooms.

And left the robot sitting and thinking his dark thoughts.

Nine

Later, it must have been close to sunset, they all gathered in Watch's bedroom. They had been wakened not long before that. Several of Neernitt's goons had come inside the house and removed all the video cameras. Apparently the robot no longer thought he needed them. Yet Adam thought the move peculiar since Neernitt was still obsessed with security.

The goons remained outside, circling the house.

The gang sat together in Watch's bedroom. Savannah sat on the bed beside Bryce. The two seemed to be hitting it off, much to the displeasure of the other girls, Cindy in particular.

But it was upon Watch that all the eyes were focused.

They just could not figure him out.

'For once we're really alone,' Adam said and he sighed. 'If the whole world becomes like this house has been the last week, I don't think I want to live in it. Knowing someone is staring over my shoulders gives me the creeps.'

'I must admit I have missed my privacy,' Sally said.

'You don't like rooming with me?' Cindy asked.

'I didn't say that. I found you to be a perfectly acceptable roommate – if you like snoring, sleep-talking people, and an assortment of other unpleasant personal habits that I feel it would be indelicate of me to talk about at this moment.'

'Well, I like you too,' Cindy muttered. 'But I don't feel like arguing right now. I want Watch to talk.'

Watch looked innocent. 'What do you want me to talk about?'

'Get off it,' Adam said angrily. 'You've sold your soul to that monster and you don't think you have to explain yourself? What was that little speech you gave in there after you activated the robot? Since when did you want to be a robot?'

Watch considered. 'I've always wanted to be a robot.'

Sally sniggered. 'Yeah. You've talked about it for years.'

Watch shook his head. 'No. I haven't been able to talk about it with you guys. I haven't been able to talk to you guys about a lot of stuff. You know that and I think that's part of the problem. That's why I think I'll do better as a robot. Then I won't have to feel things. Then there will be no need for me to talk. I can just work and do my duty.'

Adam was aghast. 'To Neernitt?'

Watch hesitated. 'If he is to be in charge, I will serve him.'

'But he's evil,' Adam complained. 'He hurts people. How can you serve him?'

'He may hurt people in the short term, but I believe his long term goals are valid. Mankind has got to evolve beyond his physical body. The body is in many ways the greatest obstacle to mankind. You said it yourself, Sally, our bodies wear out and die just when we figure out what we're doing with them. And all these emotions we have cause so many problems. We have wars and riots and poverty everywhere on this planet. But if we were all robots we could eliminate our emotions. We would all be . . . happy.'

'But how can we be happy if we have no emotions?' Cindy asked.

Watch thought before speaking. He turned to Savannah.

'What do you think of that question?' he asked her. 'Do you think it's possible to be happy while feeling nothing?'

Savannah was surprised to be the centre of attention. She withdrew her hand from Bryce's arm. She had been stroking it, almost without thinking. Bryce had not seemed to notice the attention, or if he had he hadn't seemed to mind.

Watch had caught Savannah off guard with his question. She looked distressed at being put on the spot. It made Adam wonder how little they knew about her, even after having lived in the house with her for a week. The last few days she had kept to herself. She had even made a point of having her own room. She had told them nothing about her life. Except for their initial encounter, she had not brought up her family again.

'Did you hear the question?' Watch asked. 'Do you understand?'

Savannah blinked and glanced at Bryce.

The question seemed to hurt her.

'I don't think one needs to feel to be happy,' she said.

'So you would like to be a robot as well?' Watch asked.

Again Savannah hesitated. 'Yes.'

'I knew the girl was weird,' Sally muttered.

Watch seemed satisfied with her answer.

'I think it's time we go and talk to Neernitt,' he said, and stood up.

'Who wants to talk to that creep?' Adam asked as he jumped up. 'Wait until he calls. Why go looking for more trouble? Besides, we're finally alone, Watch, I need to talk to you more. I just can't see you selling out the human race just because you have trouble expressing your emotions. It isn't like you.'

Watch spoke seriously. 'Then it shows how little you know me.' He walked towards the door. 'I really do think we should all talk to Neernitt.'

So they went to talk to Neernitt.

The robot was standing in the living room and looking out of the window. His green eyes – the ones he had stolen from Olos, Adam thought – showed no emotion. Yet Adam got the impression that he wanted to go outside. After all, the guy had been cooped up all his life online. With his robot body he could now do what he pleased and go where he wanted. Adam thought that even for a nasty robot that must be a liberating feeling.

There was a rifle on the coffee table.

'I did not call for you,' Neernitt said without turning.

Watch bowed slightly. 'If we are disturbing you we can leave.'

Neernitt turned. 'No, that is not necessary. What is it you want?'

Watch smiled. 'I want you to enjoy your robot body that I worked so hard to build for you. I want you to go outside and walk our streets and see the sky. I want you to be free of this house and all other limitations.'

Neernitt regarded him closely.

'There is a danger in that, you know. You know that very well, Watch.'

Watch acted confused. 'What's the danger? I don't understand?'

Neernitt waved a claw. He was already picking up human gestures.

'It does not matter right now. I was about to go outside. To do that I will require you to disconnect my modem lines from the Internet. But before you do that I want to settle the question of your loyalty to me. Of your dedication to the great work set before us – that of transforming all of humanity into mechanical beings.'

Watch nodded. 'I am ready and willing to do your bidding.'

Neernitt took a step forward. 'So you say. And so for the last week you have proven yourself. But a final test is required before I can trust you completely. You must show me that human life has no meaning to you.'

Watch looked uncomfortable. 'What are you suggesting?'

Neernitt picked up the rifle on the coffee table. He held it out for Watch and Watch took it. Adam knew the gun could not hurt the robot.

'Your task,' Neernitt said, 'is to convince me that

you are tired of biological forms. That your emotions no longer rule your life. You can do that by shooting one of your fellow humans in the room.' Neernitt paused. 'I do not care which one. Only that you do it within the next minute.'

'And if I refuse?' Watch asked.

Neernitt was cold. 'You do not want to refuse, Watch.'

Watch shifted the rifle in his hands and looked around at each of them. The situation was surreal – Adam couldn't grasp what was happening. It seemed that each time they got a measure of control back in their lives Neernitt would snatch it away. He truly was a wicked being and Adam wondered once again how the Internet could have given birth to him.

'I don't know which one to shoot,' Watch said.

'All humans are the same to me,' Neernitt said. 'To be like me you must view them in the same light. Just shoot one and be done with it. Your minute passes quickly.'

Watch raised the rifle to his shoulder and aimed at the wall.

The group stood paralysed.

Except for Savannah. She began to back up slightly.

They understood. She was the only one Watch didn't know well.

It would be logical to kill her. A stranger.

She had said her name was Savannah Stranger.

Logic was what mattered here. To be like a robot.

Savannah tried to turn away, to leave the room.

Watch spun in a half-circle and aimed at her chest.

Savannah froze. Stared at him. Her expression was a mystery.

'Watch,' Adam gasped. 'You can't do it.'

Watch fired the rifle. The noise was deafening.

Red blossomed in the centre of Savannah's chest.

Watch had shot her directly in the heart.

She crumpled to the floor.

'Oh no,' Cindy gasped. Sally turned her head away, tears in her eyes. Adam lowered his head, it seemed as if the weight of the world had fallen on his shoulders. Watch calmly placed the rifle back on the coffee table and spoke to Neernitt.

'I have done your bidding,' he told the robot. 'I

will always do your bidding. I hope I have gained your trust now.'

Neernitt nodded. 'It is time you disconnected my wires. It is time I walked in this world I have been chosen to rule.'

Watch approached the back of the robot's head.

'With your permission, my lord?' he asked as he touched the modem wires.

'You have my permission and my loyalty,' Neernitt said.

Watch unplugged the wires from the robot's head. The gang watched as Neernitt walked towards the front door and held out his metallic claw to turn the door handle. It was better to watch him than to look at the puddle of blood forming beneath Savannah. She had crumpled face down on the floor and was lying so still it broke Adam's heart. Watch had shot her, killed her, without blinking an eye.

For Adam the whole world had gone insane.

A dark despair settled over his heart.

Neernitt was going outside to destroy humanity.

Adam wished Watch had shot him instead.

The robot opened the door and took a step on to the porch.

'Neernitt,' Watch said calmly to his back.

The robot paused and turned. 'Yes? What is it?'

'I have something important to tell you about the design of the body you now inhabit,' Watch said. 'Now that you are disconnected from the Internet.'

Neernitt seemed annoyed, if that was possible.

'Can this information not wait until another time?' the robot asked.

Watch shook his head. 'I'm afraid it can't wait. You see, when I first figured out what you are and understood that you were unlocalised – present everywhere in a million different computers – I knew you were a being that could not be easily destroyed. In fact, as long as you remained spread out all over the world, you were *impossible* to destroy. At any moment you could move your mind through another phone line, another row of silicon chips. Who could stop such a creature, I thought? The answer was no one.' Watch paused for effect. 'Do you understand?'

Neernitt shook his bulky head. 'I do not

understand. Explain yourself quickly and clearly.'

Watch flashed a smile. 'Yes sir, I will do that. What I am trying to say, lord and master, is that you have been fooled. I suggested the idea to you of building you a robot body for one purpose only. To place your consciousness in a confined space. So that it could be dealt with. So that it could be destroyed.'

Neernitt took a step back into the house.

'You speak nonsense. I cannot be destroyed, I am immortal. It is you who will be destroyed. I will have you shot.'

Watch lost his smile. 'You will do no such thing. It is you who is to be destroyed. You watched me build this robot through three video cameras but you did not understand everything I was doing. There are two switches located inside your head behind your eyes. They are duplicates of each other – in the remote chance one should fail. These switches are activated by this device I now hold.' Watch pulled a small black box from his pocket and showed Neernitt the button on its side. 'When I push this button the switches inside your head will trigger an electrical overload. Your brains will

110

begin to fry, and since you are now disconnected from the Internet, *you* will begin to fry. You will die, Neernitt, and the world will be a better place for it.'

The robot looked positively confused.

'But why, Watch?' he asked. 'I was going to make you immortal.'

Watch laughed softly. 'To be human is to be mortal. And I like humans. I love them, I think, almost as much as I hate you.'

Watch held up the button for all to see and pushed it.

The effect was instantaneous.

The robot's eyes began to glow a frightful green colour. He backed up and banged into the half-open door. His metal claws flailed wildly. A tremor went through his whole steel form and even a trace of smoke poured out of his ears. The green of his eyes turned to red, to orange, and finally the depths of them began to sizzle with sparks pouring out of a hole of misery. A mind so evil it created its own stench. But it was a good smell because the smoke was killing the beast. Neernitt fell face first on to the floor. He twitched for a few seconds and finally went still.

The monster was dead. They had won.

Watch had saved them.

Adam felt terrible that he had doubted his friend.

But Savannah was dead. Watch had killed her.

How could they rejoice in the presence of so much blood?

'It isn't blood,' Watch said as he appeared to read their minds. He strode across the room and knelt beside Savannah. He put his hand on her bloody shoulder and shook her gently. 'Your monster is dead. You can stop pretending. You can get up now, Neernitt.'

Savannah raised her head and looked up at him.

Adam almost fainted. But he had to catch Cindy from doing likewise.

'She was working with you all along!' Adam exclaimed.

Watch shook his head. 'She was working against us all along. She is the monster. Or, I should say, she created it. Didn't you, Savannah?'

Savannah sat up and crossed her legs in the red goo.

She stared at all of them, but especially at Bryce.

'Yes,' she said quietly. 'It was me who brought Neernitt to life on the Internet. I wrote a complex program that created him.'

'But how?' Adam asked. 'Are you a computer genius or something?'

She spoke without pride. 'I am the greatest computer genius in the world.' She glanced at Watch. 'But I am not the greatest genius in the world. How did you figure it out?'

Watch also spoke without pride. 'You sometimes spoke like Neernitt. You would say, "Do you understand?" just like him. But that was not the only clue. When Neernitt almost had us all shot, you were supposedly inside here asleep. Yet when I came back inside, the computer in your room was on. You were controlling Neernitt the whole time.'

She nodded. 'I have always controlled him.'

Bryce was stunned. 'He never made you do horrible things?'

She spoke softly. 'No. *I* made him do horrible things.'

'Wait a second,' Sally complained. 'Watch just shot you. How come you're alive?'

'The gun never had real bullets in it,' Savannah

said. 'I was just testing Watch via Neernitt.'

'To see if I would really help you?' Watch asked.

'Yes.' She nodded. 'You know. You figured it out. You knew who was controlling the play. You knew I would never give you a real gun.'

Watch nodded. 'That's true. But I only knew for sure at the very end, when we talked in the room a few minutes ago.' Watch paused. 'When you looked so pained because you felt something for Bryce.'

Savannah was depressed. 'I was so obvious to you.'

Bryce spoke with feeling. 'Not to me.'

She looked at him. 'I wanted to destroy the world. I almost did it, you know.'

Bryce was wounded. He must have cared for her more than they knew.

'But why, Savannah?' he asked.

She smiled sadly. 'Maybe because I am the robot. No, not a real robot. But it is hard for me to feel things without also feeling pain.'

'All this was a set-up?' Bryce asked.

'Yes.' Savannah slowly stood and glanced at Watch again. 'But I never knew I was the one who was being set up.'

'None of us knew,' Adam said.

Watch took no pleasure in his victory.

'You have a great mind,' he told her. 'You can do great things for the world.'

'You're not going to turn me over to the police?' she asked.

'No. It would be too great a waste of your talents,' Watch said.

She nodded in appreciation. 'You are kind.'

Watch nodded. 'You were a worthy opponent.'

Savannah went to where Bryce sat with his cast.

'I'm sorry I hurt your leg,' she said.

Bryce nodded. 'It's all right, it'll heal.'

A tear ran down her cheek. 'You forgive me. You all forgive me, and after what I have done to you.'

'We want to be your friend,' Adam said.

She glanced at him. 'The friend of the young girl who tried to turn the whole world into robots? That's why I set all this up. To use Watch's talents and the rest of you. I wanted a world where no one felt anything.' She paused and turned back to Bryce. 'Where there was no pain.'

'Do you feel pain now?' he asked gently.

'Yes. It is hard to say goodbye to you.'

Bryce took her hand. 'Then don't say goodbye.' He flashed a smile. 'You still have to sign my cast.'

Sayannah managed a faint smile. 'What should I write?'

Bryce was bold. 'Your phone number.'

Savannah took a pen and knelt and scribbled her number on his cast. Then without speaking she stood and leaned over and kissed him on the cheek. But she left the house with her head held low. They all understood that she had things to work out in her life.

All of them except, perhaps, Sally.

'I wouldn't call that chick if you paid me,' Sally said.

*If you enjoyed PHONE FEAR, you'll love
Christopher Pike's other Spooksville chillers . . .*

The Witch's Gift

The witch has called Adam and the others to her castle. She's leaving Spooksville and before she goes she wants to grant them each a wish. Anything they ask for, she will give them.

But the gang must be careful what they wish for. For the witch is unpredictable as well as powerful – and behind her gift lies a hidden cost . . .

ALIENS ATE MY HOMEWORK

Bruce Coville

Do you have problems telling lies?
Can you only speak the truth – no matter how silly? Then you'll know how Rod felt when his teacher asked about his science project – because he could only tell her the truth: 'Aliens ate my homework, Miss Maloney!'

Of course, nobody believes Rod, so nobody bothers to ask where the aliens come from. Just as well – because Rod is helping Madame Pong and the crazy crew of the Ferkel on a *very* secret mission . . .

Spooksville
CHRISTOPHER PIKE

All Hodder Children's books are available at your local bookshop, or can be ordered direct from the publisher. Just tick the titles you would like and complete the details below. Prices and availability are subject to change without prior notice.

Please enclose a cheque or postal order made payable to *Bookpoint Ltd*, and send to: Hodder Children's Books, 39 Milton Park, Abingdon, OXON OX14 4TD, UK. Email Address: orders@bookpoint.co.uk

If you would prefer to pay by credit card, our call centre team would be delighted to take your order by telephone. Our direct line *01235 400414* (lines open 9.00 am–6.00 pm Monday to Saturday, 24 hour message answering service). Alternatively you can send a fax on *01235 400454*.

TITLE		FIRST NAME		SURNAME	

ADDRESS	
DAYTIME TEL:		POST CODE	

If you would prefer to pay by credit card, please complete: Please debit my Visa/Access/Diner's Card/American Express (delete as applicable) card no:

Signature ....

Expiry Date: ....

If you would NOT like to receive further information on our products please tick the box. ☐

Another Hodder Children's Book

GRAVEYARD SCHOOL 10: TERROR IN THE TOILETS

Tom B Stone

Alex Lee only wants to use the bathroom – but the doorway is glowing, it's rumbling inside and there's smoke all down the hall.

Who's laughing in the lavatory? Are those *claws* appearing out of the smoke? Is there someone else in the toilet?

Alex and his friend Park are ready for a ghost hunt – but can they flush it out before Graveyard School goes down the drain?

More alien adventures from Hodder Children's Books

Bruce Coville

❑   65115 6   Aliens Ate My Homework   £2.99
❑   65116 4   I Left My Sneakers in Dimension X £2.99
❑   65355 8   Aliens Stole My Dad   £2.99

*All Hodder Children's books are available at your local bookshop,
or can be ordered direct from the publisher. Just tick the titles you
would like and complete the details below. Prices and availability
are subject to change without prior notice.*

Please enclose a cheque or postal order made payable to
Bookpoint Ltd, and send to: Hodder Children's Books, 39
Milton Park, Abingdon, OXON OX14 4TD, UK.
Email Address: orders@bookpoint.co.uk

If you would prefer to pay by credit card, our call centre team
would be delighted to take your order by telephone. Our
direct line *01235 400414* (lines open 9.00 am–6.00 pm Monday
to Saturday, 24 hour message answering service). Alternatively
you can send a fax on *01235 400454*.

TITLE	FIRST NAME		SURNAME	
ADDRESS				
DAYTIME TEL:			POST CODE	

If you would prefer to pay by credit card, please complete:
Please debit my Visa/Access/Diner's Card/American
Express (delete as applicable) card no:

Signature ....

Expiry Date: ....

If you would NOT like to receive further information on
our products please tick the box. ❏

More spine-tingling reads from Hodder Children's Books

Laugh till you scream with

Tom B. Stone's

GRAVEYARD SCHOOL series

☐	63693 9	Deadly Dinners	£2.99
☐	63694 7	The Headless Bike Rider	£2.99
☐	63600 9	Wicked Wheels	£2.99
☐	63601 7	Little Pet Werewolf	£2.99
☐	63602 5	Revenge of the Dinosaurs	£2.99
☐	63603 3	Camp Dracula	£2.99
☐	66476 2	Slime Lake	£2.99
☐	66477 0	Terrify the Teacher!	£2.99
☐	66488 6	The Abominable Snow Monster	£2.99
☐	66489 4	Terror in the Toilets	£2.99

All Hodder Children's books are available at your local bookshop, or can be ordered direct from the publisher. Just tick the titles you would like and complete the details below. Prices and availability are subject to change without prior notice.

Please enclose a cheque or postal order made payable to *Bookpoint Ltd*, and send to: Hodder Children's Books, 39 Milton Park, Abingdon, OXON OX14 4TD, UK. Email Address: orders@bookpoint.co.uk

If you would prefer to pay by credit card, our call centre team would be delighted to take your order by telephone. Our direct line *01235 400414* (lines open 9.00 am–6.00 pm Monday to Saturday, 24 hour message answering service). Alternatively you can send a fax on *01235 400454*.

TITLE	FIRST NAME	SURNAME

ADDRESS

DAYTIME TEL:	POST CODE

If you would prefer to pay by credit card, please complete:
Please debit my Visa/Access/Diner's Card/American Express (delete as applicable) card no:

Signature ....

Expiry Date: ....

If you would NOT like to receive further information on our products please tick the box. ☐